Robert A. Purvey

Sammy & Scarlett's Coral Reef Adventure

ROBERT ANDREW PROVAN

ILLUSTRATIONS BY MARY WENTZEL

Archway Publishing books may be ordered through booksellers or by contacting:

Archway Publishing
1663 Liberty Drive
Bloomington, IN 47403
www.archwaypublishing.com
844-669-3957

Illustrations by Mary Wentzel.

ISBN: 978-1-6657-3931-3 (sc)
ISBN: 978-1-6657-3932-0 (hc)
ISBN: 978-1-6657-3930-6 (e)

Print information available on the last page.

Archway Publishing rev. date: 5/17/2023

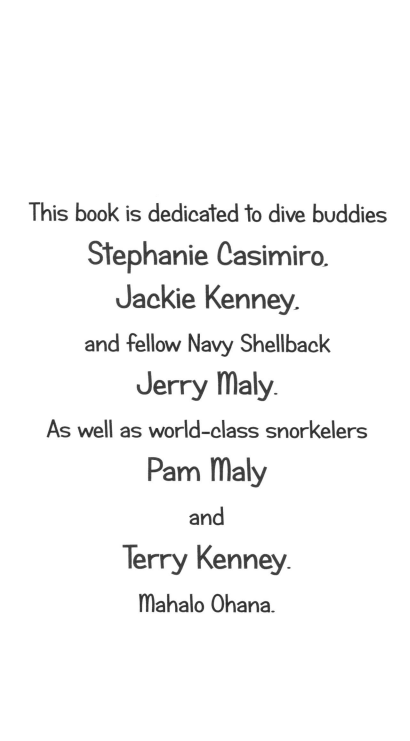

This book is dedicated to dive buddies
Stephanie Casimiro,
Jackie Kenney,
and fellow Navy Shellback
Jerry Maly.
As well as world-class snorkelers
Pam Maly
and
Terry Kenney.
Mahalo Ohana.

Other books by Robert Andrew Provan:

Ronnie the Raindrop

Sammy & Scarlett's Mangrove Adventure

Introduction

Sammy & Scarlett's Mangrove Adventure tells the story of the main characters Sammy, the sergeant major, and Scarlett, the yellowtail snapper, as they travel from their Florida Keys tidal pool home to the mangrove forest. Mangrove forests are the nurseries of the coral reef, and in the natural world, it is where many of the reef's inhabitants spend their first years of life.

Sammy and Scarlett's Coral Reef Adventure is the lively tale of two tiny fish in a very big ocean as they make the epic journey from the mangrove forest to their adult home in the reefs of the Florida Keys. With the help of their new friend Howie the hawksbill sea turtle, they must learn to deal with their new environment. The sources of danger are many, as are the natural wonders of this new place. From fearsome predators to the gentle swaying of sea fans in sun-dappled coral reefs, won't you and your family join Sammy, Scarlett, and Howie as they make this incredible journey to one of the most extraordinary places on this planet? You will be glad you did...

4

Sammy and Scarlett swam hard and fast all day as Manny had advised, always staying close to the bottom, stopping when they saw predator fish above. Whenever they found a pile of rocks or other structures, they rested a bit out of sight. The seagrass meadows held lots of food, so they ate as they went.

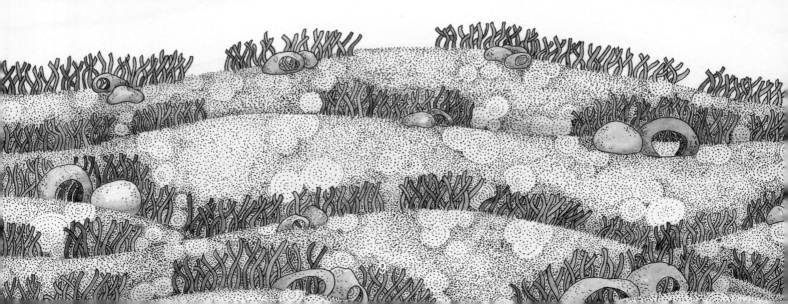

On the morning of the second day, they emerged from under an old barnacle-encrusted anchor and resumed their journey out to sea. Two things happened to help Sammy and Scarlett the second day's afternoon. The first was a strong sea current at their backs that pushed them along the seafloor toward their future home on the coral reef.

Making a new friend is almost always a good thing, and that was what happened next. A friendly hawksbill sea turtle named Howie swam down to eat some seagrass. Sammy and Scarlett saw his shadow and took cover under a rock.

"It's OK, guys. I won't hurt you. I am a sea turtle and do not eat fish. You can come out from under that rock. My name is Howie."

Timidly the two small fish poked their heads out. Scarlett said, "Hello, my name is Scarlett; I'm a yellowtail snapper. This is my best friend, Sammy, a sergeant major. We are going to the reef."

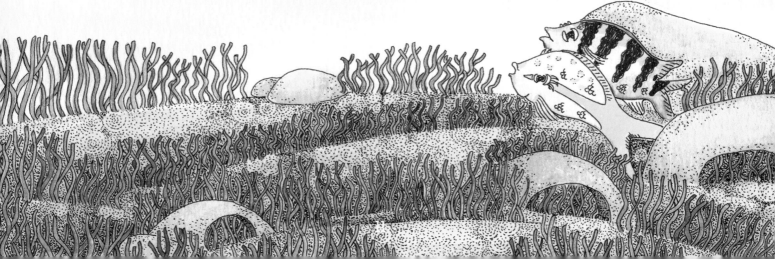

"Well, so am I. It's a pleasure to meet you both. After lunch, I swim to the cleaning stations, where tiny colorful fish pick me clean of parasites and barnacles. I would love some company on my trip to the reef. Maybe we can travel together! If you swim under me close to my tummy, most fish won't even see you. I can swim close to the bottom, so if need be, you can dart to cover on the seafloor," suggested Howie the hawksbill turtle.

Sammy and Scarlett loved the idea. Traveling together just made sense, so the three friends talked about how they would travel. Howie needed to go to the surface for air sometimes. Then, when he required air, the two little fish could swim up to the surface with Howie or hide on the sea bottom until he came back down for them.

"Sometimes I like to snack on the weedlines," explained Howie.

"That's OK, Howie. Sammy and I know all about the weedlines. We traveled under one for two days to reach the mangroves," said Scarlett.

Sammy said, "Yes, sir. Good cover and plenty of food on those weedlines."

Early that evening, Howie, Scarlett, and Sammy took refuge in a small patch reef for the night. "This small reef is my home base, guys," said Howie. "But I swim out to the other reefs for food, to visit cleaning stations, and to meet my girlfriend, Hannah. We can be out on the main reef by lunchtime tomorrow if we get an early start in the morning. Always remember—late in the afternoon, when the sun is low in the sky, the barracudas and sharks begin feeding. You must always seek hiding places late in the day and at night, or you may be eaten."

Scarlett always had questions, so she asked, "What other predators do we need to worry about on the reef?"

"Great question. You need to be aware of much bigger fish such as grouper, jacks, snapper, and even dolphins sometimes. Different animals eat at different times of the day. Be alert all the time," advised Howie.

"We understand because Manny the mangrove gave us the same advice often when we lived with him," exclaimed Sammy. "It makes sense, too, because Scarlett and I are still pretty small. You are a big turtle, though; I bet nobody messes with you, Howie."

"Well, huge sharks, especially tiger sharks, eat sea turtles much larger than me. Plus, many of my kind die each year from the big fishing nets humans use to catch fish and shrimp and from eating plastic bags that we mistake for jellyfish," said Howie, sighing. "We are all safe here for the night. So let's get some rest. We have a big day tomorrow, my friends."

After swimming to Howie's patch reef, the three friends had no trouble drifting off to sleep.

A deep rumbling sound woke Sammy and Scarlett up. "What was that?" asked Scarlett.

"Sorry, guys; that was me. My tummy's hungry," said Howie.

"That's OK, Howie. We are hungry too," said Sammy, laughing.

Howie's patch reef sat in only twenty feet of water, so the sunrise's blazing orange rays carried through the crystal-clear water to light up everything on the small reef.

"Looks like another beautiful morning," said Howie. "So let's all swim out to the barrier reef. We can find breakfast on the way there."

They headed out together. Howie's rumbling tummy scared away little minnows in their path as they swam.

"Oh, look up ahead, on the surface—jellyfish, my favorite!" said Howie as he swam up for his breakfast. Howie was right where a bunch of jellyfish were floating peacefully on the surface. He was hungry and very excited to see something to eat.

Sammy and Scarlett looked up from the bottom, watching their friend enjoying his breakfast. Sammy began foraging for small animals to eat in the soft corals on the bottom. Scarlett sometimes had feelings about dangerous things before they happen, and she had saved Sammy and herself more than once. Scarlett had one of these thoughts now, but she couldn't decide what was wrong with Howie on the surface. Then, suddenly, she saw it—a *plastic bag* was floating up with the jellyfish!

"Howie, *stop*!" she yelled. "Don't eat that bag!" Manny the mangrove had warned both fish about what happens to sea turtles who eat plastic bags. Howie could not hear her, but Sammy could, and he was a faster swimmer than Scarlett. So he swam as fast as lightning to the surface to warn Howie.

Howie was about to eat the bag when Sammy snatched it away and took it out of his reach.

"Why did you take my jellyfish?" asked Howie.

"That's not a jellyfish. That's a plastic bag from the humans," said Scarlett. "Sammy just saved your life the plastic bag looked like a jellyfish."

Howie put his flippers around Sammy and Scarlett. "I can never thank you both enough for saving me," he said with a shaky voice and a tear in his eye.

"I couldn't have done it without Scarlett. She saw the bag, not me," said Sammy excitedly.

Scarlett, Sammy, and Howie swam toward the main barrier reef after the plastic bag incident.

The seascape began to change as the three friends drew closer to the reef. There were beautiful bright-purple objects, which Howie said were sea fans. The sea fans swayed gently in the sunlit tropical currents. Because the water was very clear, they could see sea fans far ahead along with an increasing number of other sea creatures. The scene ahead showed the outline of the coral reef structure.

Scarlett and Sammy saw more corals, and Howie patiently named them as they swam past. There were elkhorn, brain, and star corals. All were surrounded by and full of sea life. Thousands of brightly covered fish swam everywhere. Some fish swam in tight groups called schools. Each school member seemed to know what the others were thinking, because they swam as one—changing directions and avoiding obstacles altogether moving seamlessly. Howie explained that this was to confuse big predator fish such as barracuda, jacks, and sharks.

Other fish swam alone or in small groups of two or three. Stoplight parrotfish, for example, would swim along peacefully, nibbling on coral from the reef. As Scarlett, Sammy, and Howie stopped to watch the parrotfish, it dawned on Scarlett that the reef was a noisier place than the tidal pool or the mangrove forests of her youth.

She could clearly hear the parrotfish munching on the coral, as well as a myriad of other clicking and grunting sounds from other reef animals. Scarlett and Sammy would learn what all the sounds meant as time passed. Inhabitants of the reef made noises to mark their territory, attract a mate, or warn of danger, such as intruders approaching.

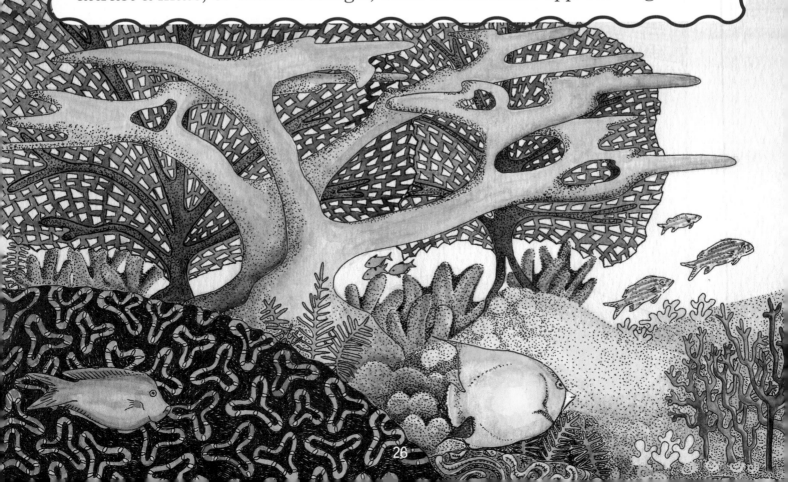

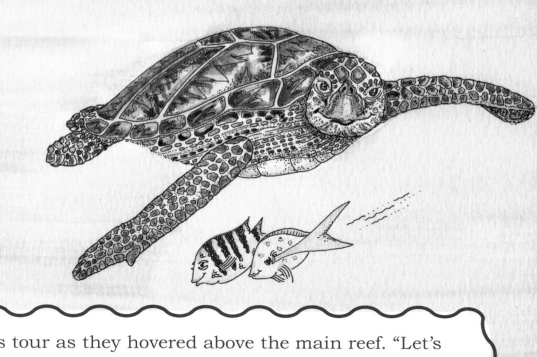

Howie continued his tour as they hovered above the main reef. "Let's swim this way," he said. "Please stay close to me; there are a few things I want to show you."

They swam northward along the reef, which teemed with vibrant life below them. Scarlett noticed twenty or so yellowtail snapper swim past. Sammy also kept seeing sergeant majors darting by, seemingly chasing each other for fun.

"Scarlett and Sammy, you will see many of your kind here. Some but not all will become your friends. Here in the natural world, some fish will become your competition, and some will become your enemies," said Howie in a confident voice.

As they swam along the top of the reef, the view was amazing! Fish of every color, size, and shape darted through the corals and sponges that Scarlett and Sammy had just learned about from Howie. The turtle, who always seemed hungry, had just eaten several sponges off the reef for an early lunch. Scarlett and Sammy had noticed lots of small fish darting from inside the colorful sponges. While some sponges on the reef were tan or cream-colored, others were red, orange, or yellow. The fish and small animals that lived within the sponges were just as colorful. Scarlett and Sammy found that they were also delicious for lunch.

Howie pointed out predators as they swam along; the two small fish stayed close to Howie, who seemed to know everyone and everything about life on the barrier reef.

Gray reef and blacktip sharks glided past, paying no attention to the three friends. The big, thick-bodied bull sharks they soon passed were less graceful but far scarier. The bulls turned to watch. Howie said, "Stay away from all sharks as much as you can. When you see them coming, take cover. Look ahead— see that big silver fish up there? He's a barracuda and just as dangerous as any shark!"

"He is not as big as the sharks," said Sammy excitedly.

"No, but look at those teeth!" said Scarlett as they drew nearer.

"Time is on our side. Barracuda like to eat later in the day when the sun is lower in the sky. Now, with the sun right above us, the barracuda sit almost motionless, watching the reef's inhabitants go about their day. When a barracuda does decide to attack, they are fast as lightning!" explained Howie. "A good way to stay safe is to watch the behavior of other fish and animals and stay close to cover, like the reef or rocks. Inhabitants of the reef work together in ways that are clear to those of us paying attention. Predators don't scare just one fish on the reef, so when you see other fish taking cover, do so yourself."

"That makes sense," said Scarlett. "Remember when we were baby fish in our tidal pool, Sammy? Whenever anyone saw a heron or egret sneaking up to the pool, we all hid."

"That's right; I do remember that," said Sammy excitedly.

"It's the same thing. In this way, even a fish who is your enemy might save your life by alerting you to danger approaching that they may have seen first," stated Howie.

Soon they came to a canyon formed when one section of the reef ended and, about the length of a gray reef shark away, another reef area started. In the gap between could be seen an orderly line of fish. They all seemed polite, swimming nose to tail; no one was cutting in line, and no fish were fighting or chasing each other.

"Howie, what is going on down there?" asked Scarlett.

"Ah, time for a pit stop. That, my young friends, is a cleaning station; everyone comes here to get cleaned and groomed by small wrasse. Watch the fish at the head of the line. See the tiny colorful fish swimming in and out of his mouth, between his gills, and over his skin? The little wrasse are removing parasites and other items. The big fish get cleaned, and the tiny cleaner fish get a meal. Everyone behaves at the cleaning stations, even sharks and barracuda! Why don't you guys look around a bit while I get in line to have my shell cleaned? Stay close by where you can see me, please," said Howie.

Scarlett and Sammy watched as Howie got in line at the cleaning station.

"Do you believe how polite everyone is here, Sammy?" asked Scarlett.

"It seems that everyone must follow the rules at the cleaning station. But I think once they leave, Scarlett, it's back to eat or be eaten," said Sammy, sighing.

The two fish had no way of knowing that one resident of the reef never followed the rules at the cleaning station.

"Oh, look! Howie is getting his shell cleaned!" exclaimed Scarlett.

"Yeah, those wrasse look pretty plump and tasty," said Sammy, chuckling.

In the shadows of a coral cave behind the two young fish lurked a fish who was never full. This type of fish was never welcomed at the cleaning station. Slowly this intruder left the shadows, approaching from behind. This was a lionfish, beautiful but very deadly to all fish. He silently drew closer to Scarlett and Sammy. Scarlett noticed other fish looking toward them and then very quickly darting for cover. Instinctively, she turned around.

"Quick, Sammy, swim for it!" cried Scarlett, her heart racing.

Sammy had not yet turned around but followed his friend as she very quickly swam deeper into the canyon.

The lionfish was right behind them, snapping his jaws in an attempt to bite them.

"Take cover, Scarlett," said Sammy. "I will keep swimming. That fish can't catch me!"

Scarlett was out of breath, and she knew that Sammy was a much faster swimmer. Reluctantly she said, "OK, on three we split up."

"One, two, three!" said both fish. Scarlett darted to the left, into an opening in the coral, while Sammy sped up and went to the right.

To their horror, the big lionfish went left in pursuit of Scarlett!

"Hey, leave her alone!" yelled Sammy as he raced toward the much bigger lionfish, unsure what he could do to help her. Before he could reach the lionfish, however, something big knocked him aside.

It was Howie, who grabbed the lionfish by the tail and pulled him away from where Scarlett was hiding. Howie was angry; he shook the lionfish hard and then banged him against the reef.

Once Howie let go of the lionfish, it floated belly up to the sea bottom. They saw the larger stinging fins draw close to the body of the lionfish. From the base of the reef, a large green moray eel came out, grabbed the dead lionfish, and dragged him back into his small cave.

"Is everyone OK?" asked Scarlett from her hiding place within the corals.

"Yes, Scarlett, thanks to Howie—he just saved both our lives," said Sammy.

"You can come out now, Scarlett; the coast is clear. I think that we have had enough excitement for one day. Let's make our way back to my patch reef," said Howie.

"Great idea, Howie; I like the safety of your reef," responded Sammy.

"Me too," said Scarlett. "I feel safe there."

"Stay close by me. The bigger fish will stay away if you do," said Howie.

The three friends swam back across the same stretch of reef. Scarlett and Sammy were not talking. They were watching the view below, taking in the sites and sand, and learning just by watching the natural world around them.

"There is something else I need to show you. Look up ahead," said Howie.

"Why is the coral white? What happened to it?" asked Scarlett.

"The seas are warming. Those white corals are dead. It's called coral bleaching. All through the great oceans, coral bleaching is happening. But the news isn't all bad," explained Howie.

"Well, it sure sounds bad," said Sammy.

"Look ahead—see those elkhorn corals?" asked Howie.

"Yes, they are beautiful," said Scarlett.

"Those were planted there by humans," said Howie.

"No way, Howie! Humans litter and throw plastic bags in the water," said Sammy.

"Well, you are right that some humans do those things and worse, but many other humans try to help nature."

"Manny the mangrove taught us that when we lived in the mangrove forest," said Scarlett, sighing.

"Manny is usually right, and he is this time too," said Howie. "I have known him for many years. Humans have planted thousands of baby corals here in the Florida Keys."

"Humans sure seem complicated," said Scarlett.

"They are. Humans are just another kind of animal. Like us, no two are the same. Well, let's head to my reef. It's good to get settled in before the big predators start getting hungry."

"Agreed, Howie. My tummy is rumbling," said Sammy.

"You are always hungry, Sammy," said Scarlett, laughing.

THE END

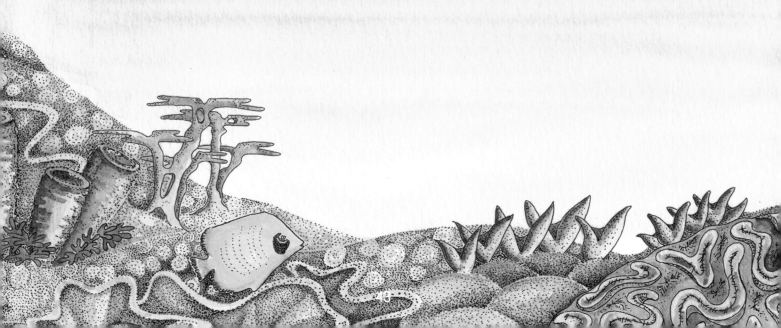